CRAFTY CHAMELEON

2016

Other books by Mwenye Hadithi and Adrienne Kennaway:

Lazy Lion
Hot Hippo
Greedy Zebra
Hungry Hyena
Tricky Tortoise

A catalogue record of this book is available from the British Library.

ISBN 0 340 48698 8

Text copyright © Bruce Hobson 1987
Illustrations copyright © Adrienne Kennaway 1987

The right of Bruce Hobson and Adrienne Kennaway to be identified
as the author and illustrator of this Work has been asserted by them
in accordance with the Copyright, Designs and Patents Act 1988.

First published 1987
This edition published 2004

20 19 18 17 16 15 14 13 12 11 10

Published by Hodder Children's Books
a division of Hodder Headline Limited
338 Euston Road, London NW1 3BH

Printed and bound in Hong Kong

CRAFTY CHAMELEON

By
Mwenye Hadithi

Illustrated by
Adrienne Kennaway

Hodder
Children's
Books

a division of Hodder Headline Limited

Every morning Chameleon rested
and caught flies in the high
branches of the Mugumu tree.

Every morning
Leopard came jumping
and leaping from branch
to branch, landing beside
Chameleon with a heavy

THUD!

And Chameleon then bounced high into the air, going around and around and around, until he hit the ground with a

SMACK!

One day Chameleon
shouted angrily:
"If you don't leave me alone I shall
tie you up with a rope, like a dog!"

"Hah!" laughed Leopard.
And he bounced away.

Now, every evening Chameleon
walked to the river to drink with
the other small animals.

Every evening, Crocodile came swishing
and slithering out of the water,
snakking his teeth and laughing as
all the small animals ran away.

One day Chameleon shouted angrily: "If you don't leave me alone I shall tie you up with a rope, like a dog!"

"Hah hah hah!" laughed the Crocodile, shutting his teeth with a great big

SNAKK!

So Chameleon asked the Weaving
Birds to weave him a rope of convolvulus
vines, and disguised himself as a stone.
And when Leopard came bouncing along,
Chameleon threw the rope round his neck, calling:
"Now I have you on a rope I shall pull you along!
Just wait until I pull."

Leopard waited, laughing, for he knew the
tiny Chameleon couldn't pull him.

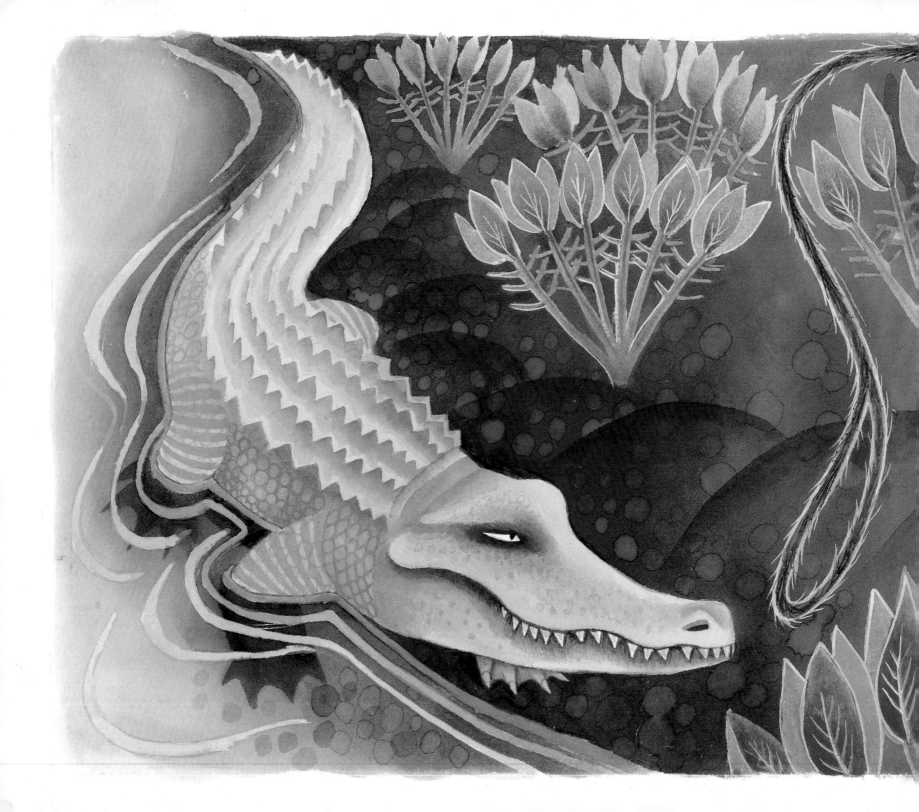

Chameleon
took the other end
of the rope down to
the river, and disguised
himself as a branch.
And when Crocodile came slithering along, Chameleon
threw the rope round his neck, calling: "Now I have you
on a rope I shall pull you along! Just wait until I pull."

"I'll wait," laughed Crocodile.

And Chameleon walked back to the middle of the
rope where he could just see Crocodile to the
right. And he could just see Leopard to the left.
And Chameleon became the same colour as a leaf
so they could not see him, and yelled "Pull!"

Leopard pulled first, and Crocodile came whizzing
and splashing backwards through the mud,
his little legs whirring around and around.

Then Crocodile pulled hard, and Leopard was dragged through a nest of biting ants.

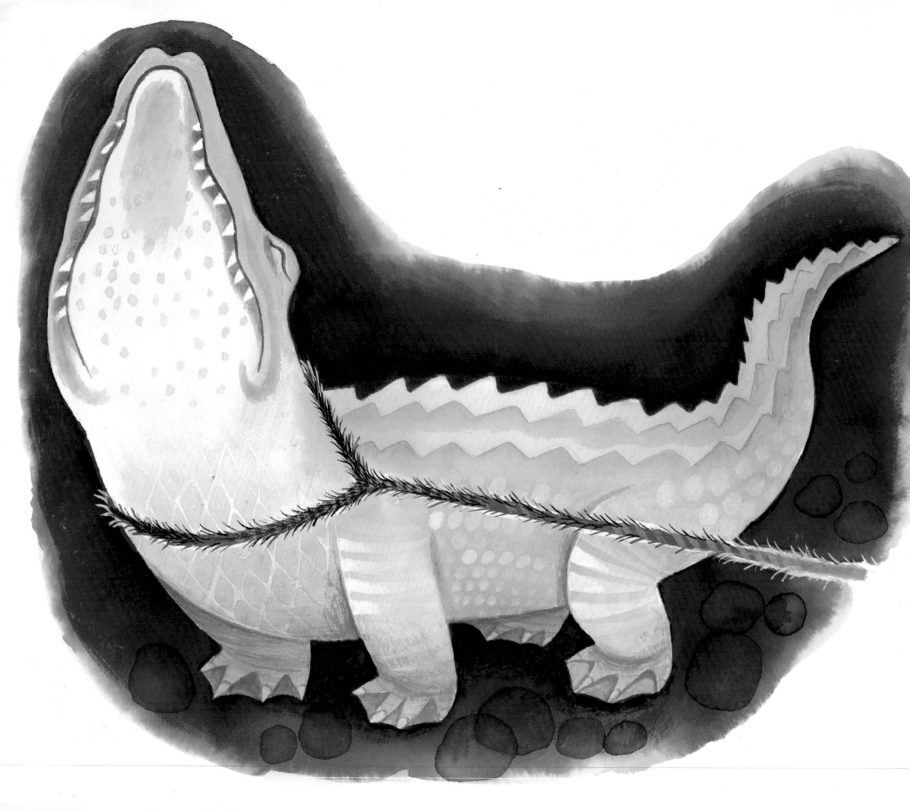

Then Leopard pulled... then Crocodile... then Leopard.
Until both animals were exhausted from
being dragged all over the forest.

"I am sorry, Mr Chameleon, I will never bother you again, I promise!" they each called. "Please let me go." And when they sat down panting, Chameleon came and cut them free.

And to this day, Crocodile and Leopard do not bother Chameleon. They leave him alone. For brains are often better than strength or size.

And Chameleon can go as slow as he likes. But just in case one of the animals finds out about the trick he played, he changes colour and hides when he hears you coming.

That is the end.